DARK DESIRES

CELESTE HAYES

Contents

1

CHAPTER 1

Nora had always been good at lying. Or perhaps, Ethan was simply too gullible.

"Why don't we have a photo together?" Ethan asked innocently during dinner, his brows slightly furrowed. It was a simple enough question, but Nora had prepared for it.

"Because you've been camera shy, baby," she cooed, leaning over to peck his forehead softly. She quickly diverted his attention by placing a plate of food in front of him. His food.

Ethan's eyes wandered to the glass of dark red liquid by his plate. He lifted it to his lips, hesitating for only a moment before taking a sip. Instantly, a rush of energy coursed through his veins. His body craved more.

"What is this juice?" he asked, taking another gulp, his eyes lighting up with hunger he couldn't quite understand.

"It's your medicine," Nora replied, her smile never wavering as she sat across from him. She was pleased. Ethan never questioned her—he believed every word she said, and that trust was intoxicating.

They ate in awkward silence, the only sound being the clinking of cutlery against their plates. Nora's eyes rarely left him. She studied his every move—his jawline, his eyes, his raw power. Ethan was perfect.

Her creation, designed exactly as she wanted.

"Eat up, baby," she purred, her voice sweet but firm. "You've got work tomorrow. It's been months."

"You said I'm a police officer, right?" Ethan asked, still trying to grasp at the shadows of his memory, but there was nothing. Just an empty void.

"That's right, honey," Nora responded smoothly. "And I'm in the forensic department, same building. I'll be there with you." She reached across the table to take his hand, her touch deliberate and possessive.

Despite her words, Ethan felt a strange unease creeping into him. He stared into Nora's eyes, but what he saw wasn't love or comfort. It was something else—something distant and unfamiliar. He couldn't shake the feeling that he didn't really know her.

The next morning, they left for work together. To his surprise, the moment Ethan stepped into the police station, everyone greeted him with warmth and concern, asking about his health and how he'd been. It was overwhelming. His instincts kicked in, a sudden hunger gnawing at him. He had an intense urge to sink his teeth into their necks, to feel their blood on his tongue.

Nora sensed it. She tightened her grip on his hand. "Smile," she whispered in his ear, her breath warm against his skin. And like the obedient creation he was, Ethan did what he was told.

Days turned into weeks, and Ethan slowly adjusted to his life. But something between him and Nora felt off. They shared a bed, but their intimacy felt forced, almost scripted. Despite her beauty, they had never gone beyond simple touches. Nora, for her part, seemed perfectly content with the distance.

One evening, as Nora sat on their bed, her nose buried in a thick book, Ethan's curiosity finally got the better of him.

"What are you reading?" he asked, turning towards her, his voice casual.

"A book about vampires," she said with a soft chuckle, not bothering to lift her gaze from the page. Her words seemed almost too casual, as though they held a secret Ethan couldn't quite grasp.

Ethan's hand slid under the sheet, gently brushing against her bare thigh. She was wearing red lingerie—tempting, seductive, the kind of sight that stirred something primal in him. He thought maybe this was her way of inviting him closer, that she wanted more. And after everything, he owed her.

"What are you doing?" Nora whispered, her voice catching slightly as she placed the book aside. Ethan's fingers trailed higher, pausing just beneath the thin fabric of her lacy panties.

"You want this, don't you?" he murmured, his breath hot against her skin as he moved aside the lingerie and slipped two fingers inside her. The tightness gripped him, and he could feel her body tremble in response.

"B-babe," Nora breathed, her eyes closing as her hands gripped the sheets. Before she could say anything more, Ethan's lips were on hers, his hand gripping the back of her neck as he deepened the kiss, his other hand moving in rhythm with her body.

But then, Nora broke the kiss, her eyes locking onto his, her breathing heavy. Her fingers brushed against his jawline, her voice soft yet firm.

"You're not ready yet," she whispered, brushing her lips gently against his again before pulling back.

Ethan was confused, but he wasn't angry. He let her go, retreating into his thoughts, unsure of what exactly had just happened.

The next day, as Ethan sat alone in their home, still trying to make sense of the night before, he heard a soft whimper. He turned to see the neighbor's golden retriever sitting by the back door, its big, innocent eyes staring up at him.

"Hey, buddy," Ethan said softly, kneeling down to pet the dog. Its tail wagged as it licked his face affectionately. "Let's get you home, huh?" He smiled, but that smile slowly faded.

He didn't take the dog home. Instead, his instincts took over.

Nora watched everything unfold through the hidden cameras. She smiled to herself as she watched Ethan drain the dog's blood in the backyard, burying the lifeless body in the dirt.

"Everything is going according to plan," she whispered, her grin widening. Her monster was becoming exactly what she needed him to be.

2

CHAPTER 2

Ethan always felt a certain coldness from Nora, a distance he could never quite close. Sometimes, he doubted if she ever truly loved him. And there was something darker gnawing at him—a secret craving he couldn't escape. He was addicted to drinking raw blood. Never human—at least not yet. But he knew if the moment came, it wouldn't surprise him.

One night during patrol, Ethan came across two thugs groping a woman in a dimly lit alley. Instinct took over. He stepped out of his vehicle, hand resting on his gun.

"Let her go," he ordered, voice calm but threatening. "I've got a weapon, and I won't hesitate to use it."

The woman struggled, her voice caught in her throat, her eyes pleading for help.

"You think we're scared of you, officer?" one of the men sneered, pulling out his own gun. The other thug followed suit.

They had no idea who they were dealing with.

Ethan's superhuman speed kicked in, and in a blur of movement, the fight was over before they even realized it had begun. One of the thugs collapsed, bleeding heavily. The scent of fresh blood hit Ethan like a tidal wave. He felt his pulse quicken, his hunger waking up—the raw, primal urge that he barely kept at bay.

He lost control.

In an instant, he was on the injured man, his fangs sinking into the warm flesh, drinking deep until the man's body went limp. The other thug had already run for his life, leaving the woman alone with the scene unfolding before her eyes.

"What the—" the girl gasped, her voice trembling, "Are you- a vampire?"

Ethan froze, realizing what he'd just done. He turned slowly to face her, expecting to see fear or horror in her eyes. But instead, there was neither. She wasn't scared. Not in the slightest. If anything, she seemed- intrigued.

"I'm Ava," she said, stepping forward with a smile, offering her hand like she hadn't just witnessed a murder. "Thank you for saving me, Officer-?"

"Ethan. Ethan Kings," he muttered, still trying to make sense of her calm demeanor. "Listen, can you just- never speak of this?"

"I won't," she said softly, with a little nod, her smile almost childlike. "I promise."

She was beautiful, with soft, gentle features that felt like a breath of fresh air compared to Nora's sharp, almost intimidating presence.

"Let me take you home, Ava," Ethan said, his voice softening for the first time that night. It was strange, but there was something about her that made him relax, as if the weight of his guilt momentarily lifted.

"I'd like that," she said, her eyes twinkling. "I love the way you say my name."

He pretended not to notice the playful wink she shot at him. As they drove through the quiet streets, Ava talked non-stop, her voice light and full of energy. She was a chatterbox, and Ethan found himself actually enjoying the conversation. It was a welcome distraction from the chaos in his head.

When they finally pulled up to her home—a large, elegant mansion—she scribbled her number on a piece of paper and handed it to him.

"Text me, will you?" she teased, leaning in with a mischievous smile. "I might need saving again, Officer."

"We'll see," he said, trying to keep his tone casual, though he couldn't help but notice how close she was.

Then, without warning, she leaned in and kissed him. It was quick, fleeting, but enough to leave him stunned. And he didn't pull away.

When he finally returned home, guilt flooded him. Nora was already asleep, lying peacefully beside him, completely unaware of what had just transpired. He stared at her, feeling the weight of the night settle in. Ava's warmth lingered in his thoughts, and it sickened him.

"This is wrong," he whispered, brushing a strand of hair away from Nora's face and gently kissing her lips. He swore to himself that he wouldn't betray her—not again.

The next morning, Ethan made breakfast for Nora. She looked at him, astonished.

"Babe?" she asked, smiling in surprise. "It's not my birthday, and it's definitely not our anniversary. What's going on?"

"Just wanted to do something for us," Ethan said, his hands cradling her face as he kissed her with a fierce tenderness. "Can't I?"

Nora's eyes lingered on him all through breakfast. She wasn't stupid—she could sense the change. Something was off, but she couldn't put her finger on it.

Days passed, and though Nora tried to figure out what had shifted, she couldn't find anything suspicious. But in her mind, she believed Ethan was finally falling for her.

She couldn't have been more wrong.

Ethan met Ava again. And this time, she wasn't going to let him slip away.

"You never texted me," she said, her tone laced with mock hurt.

Ethan avoided her eyes. "Do I even know you?" he asked, trying to sound indifferent.

Ava grinned. "Of course you do. You're my Mr. Vampire."

Ethan's eyes widened, panic flashing across his face. He grabbed her arm and pulled her into his car, shutting the door with a slam.

"I told you never to bring that up again," he growled, his voice low and dangerous.

Ava giggled, completely unfazed. "Oops. My bad." She leaned back in her seat, her lips curving into a smirk. "Why didn't you text me?"

"I have a girlfriend," Ethan stated firmly, trying to keep the conversation under control.

Ava's smile faltered, disappointment flickering in her eyes. "Does she know you're a vampire?"

"No," Ethan admitted, his voice tinged with bitterness. "And I don't plan to tell her."

"If she really loves you, she wouldn't care," Ava said softly, her words sinking into him. Ethan doubted Nora would ever accept that part of him—hell, he wasn't even sure she truly loved him.

"Do you love her?" Ava pressed, studying his face.

Ethan hesitated, the uncertainty weighing heavily on him. "I don't know," he confessed. "She's beautiful, but- there's always been something off between us. It doesn't feel right."

Before he could say anything more, Ava kissed him. This time, he didn't resist. He kissed her back, feeling a rush of emotion he hadn't felt in a long time. Butterflies erupted in his chest, and for the first time in a while, something felt right.

But then, reality hit him.

"This is wrong, Ava," he murmured, pulling away.

"It's not wrong if you don't love her," Ava whispered, taking his hand and placing it over her heart, where he could feel it pounding beneath her skin.

Ethan was torn. Caught between what was right and what he truly wanted.

3

CHAPTER 3

Ethan wrestled with a deep sense of guilt after betraying Nora.

He knew how much she had done for him, how much she had sacrificed, but he couldn't deny the pull Ava had over him. It was like a force he couldn't resist, one that kept drawing him in.

Ava understood him in ways he couldn't explain, and more than that, he wanted to protect her. From the world, from her abusive husband, the Mayor, Jeffrey Coopland.

"He hit me again," Ava whispered, lifting her hair to reveal the deep bruise along her jawline. Her blue eyes brimmed with unshed tears. Ethan's fingers traced the outline of the bruise, gentle and careful, as though he could wipe away the pain she felt.

"File a complaint against him, Ava. You can't keep living like this," Ethan urged, his voice steady but soft. Yet, Ava's tears flowed freely, shaking her head as she pressed her face into his chest.

"I'm scared, Ethan." Her voice trembled as her hands gripped his shirt. "He'll kill me if I do. He'll make me disappear like the others."

Ethan didn't hug her back, but his heart clenched for her. Despite his reservations, he couldn't turn his back on her suffering. The vulnerability in her eyes, the fear in her voice, all of it made him feel responsible for her.

"I'll protect you, Ava," he said firmly, lifting her chin so she could look into his eyes. "But you have to stand up for yourself."

Ava's response was swift, her lips pressing against his before he could stop her. Ethan tensed, instinctively pulling away, but the taste of her lips lingered. He resisted, tried to pull back, but Ava's hands were already undoing his fly.

"Ava, no," he whispered, his breath uneven as he tried to resist. "I can't do this to No—"

She silenced him with another kiss, her breath warm and heavy against his mouth. "Please," she moaned, her hand slipping inside, teasing him.

Ethan felt his control slipping, his body betraying him, and in the heat of the moment, he found himself imagining Nora. How it would feel if it were her.

The car filled with wet, obscene noises, Ava's head bobbing up and down, her tongue working skillfully on his little organ. When Ethan felt himself reaching the edge, Ava suddenly stopped, pulling away. He gasped, his eyes wide with confusion.

"Ava?" he questioned, his body aching with the abrupt halt. But she didn't answer.

Instead, she climbed onto his upright thing, straddling him, slipping her panties off and positioning herself above him.

"You're so big, Ethan," she moaned, lowering herself onto him. "Fuck me like you mean it."

Ethan's body moved on autopilot, responding to Ava's every command, but his mind was somewhere else.

The entire time, all he could see was Nora. Her face, her warmth, the way her body would feel against his. Guilt gnawed at him, even as Ava rode him, and the pleasure surged through him.

When it was over, Ava leaned forward and kissed him, her lips soft but demanding. "That was the best sex of my life," she whispered, smiling, before pulling away to get dressed.

Ethan remained silent, staring blankly out of the window. He couldn't bring himself to admit that he hadn't been with her at all, not really.

"It was the first and the last time, Ava," he said quietly, guilt heavy in his voice.

Ava's smile faded. "What do you mean? You didn't like it?"

"I didn't like it," Ethan repeated, harsher this time. The weight of his guilt, of the betrayal, was crushing him. He couldn't believe he'd let this happen.

Ava's face hardened, her playful demeanor evaporating. Without another word, she climbed out of the car, flipping him off as she slammed the door. "Get lost, Ethan!" she shouted, storming off down the street."Fuck you-"

Ethan watched her disappear, his mind spinning. He didn't chase after her. Instead, he drove away, his heart pounding in his chest.

When he returned home, Nora was waiting for him, the dining table set as though nothing had changed. But Ethan could see the suspicion in her eyes.

"Rough day at work?" she asked, her voice calm but searching.

"Yeah," he muttered, rubbing his neck. "I just- I feel off."

"That's normal," Nora said, her voice softening as she moved closer to him. "Your accident was bad, Ethan. You're still recovering."

Ethan blinked, caught off guard by the worry in her voice.

"I almost lost you- and it was hard for- for me." she sounded genuinely scared, like she was on the verge of losing him. He could see the tears forming in her eyes, her façade cracking just slightly.

Without thinking, Ethan moved at super speed, brushing away her tears. "Shh," he whispered, pulling her close. "I'm not leaving you, Nora. I promise."

Nora smiled weakly, her hands clutching his shirt as she buried her face in his chest. "I know you won't," she murmured, her voice barely audible.

But deep down, Nora knew. She knew about Ava. About the affair. And while Ethan thought the guilt would drive him away, Nora had already made up her mind. She wasn't going to let anyone, especially Ava, come between them.

Nora had already started planning. She would be rid of Ava, once and for all. Ethan was hers—whether he knew it or not.

The next day at work, Ethan's entire world threatened to come crashing down when Jeffrey Coopland, the mayor, walked into his office.

Coopland wasn't there for any official matter, and the look on his face said it all—he knew about the affair.

"Mr. Kings," Jeffrey said with a smug politeness as his body-guard pulled out a chair for him. He sat down slowly, like a king surveying his kingdom.

Ethan didn't flinch, keeping his composure. "How can I help you, sir?" His voice was steady, but inside, a storm was brewing. He didn't want any trouble, especially not when Nora was just down the hall, potentially within earshot.

"You've already helped me plenty, officer," Jeffrey chuckled, his laugh echoing like a villain straight out of a nightmare. He leaned forward, eyes dark with amusement. Ethan didn't break his gaze, though. He wasn't rattled, at least not outwardly.

But before Jeffrey could say more, Nora stepped into the room, her timing impeccable.

"Mr. Mayor," she greeted with a radiant smile, cutting through the tension like a blade. Ethan's eyes locked onto her, unable to hide his admiration for her confidence.

"What brings you here?" she asked, walking up next to Ethan with her head held high, her presence commanding. Jeffrey's eyes scanned her from head to toe, his once sour expression twisting into amusement.

"Just some business with Officer Kings," Jeffrey replied, standing up and, to Ethan's horror, pulling Nora into a hug. Ethan's fists clenched at his sides, jaw tight as fury bubbled inside him. How dare he touch her like that?

"Nora, leave us," Ethan commanded sharply, the authority in his voice unmistakable. He was barely holding back his rage, but he wanted her out of the room before things escalated.

But before she could respond, Jeffrey's laugh cut through the tension like a knife. "It's not just between us," he said, his grin widening as he glanced at Nora, his gaze lingering too long on her body.

Ethan's confusion deepened. "What do you mean?"

"If you lend me your girlfriend for a night," Jeffrey began, his eyes locked on Nora with a predatory hunger, "I'll forget about you and Ava ever happening."

The words hung in the air, each syllable seething with malice. Ethan felt a white-hot rage build inside him, and it took every ounce of restraint not to lunge at Jeffrey. His hands trembled, his vision narrowing to the smug face of the man before him. He wanted nothing more than to tear him apart.

Unbeknownst to Ethan, Nora wasn't shocked by Jeffrey's proposition. In fact, a glint of satisfaction danced behind her eyes. She stood there calmly, almost entertained.

After all, she was the one who had tipped off Jeffrey about his wife's affair with Ethan.

4

CHAPTER 4

Ethan's patience had snapped.

The air between him and Jeff was thick with tension as he stormed up to the mayor, grabbing him by the collar. His voice was low, dangerous. "Mr. Mayor, this is between the two of us. Leave Nora out of it, or you'll regret it."

Before Ethan could do anything more, Nora rushed in, her voice pleading. "Ethan, stop! Let him go."

Her words pulled Ethan back, the fire in him dimming, but just barely. She stepped between them, her wide eyes full of confusion and concern. "There must be some mistake. Ethan wouldn't do something like this."

His heart twisted at her unwavering trust. The guilt gnawed at him like a blade slowly carving into his chest. How could she trust him so blindly?

Jeff's laughter broke the silence, cruel and mocking. "Mistake?" He sneered, brushing off his jacket. "Why don't you ask your boyfriend about that?"

Nora turned to Ethan, eyes searching for the denial she so desperately needed. But he couldn't meet her gaze. His head hung low, shame weighing him down like a ton of bricks. His silence spoke volumes.

Nora said nothing. She didn't need to. The hurt on her face was enough. Without a word, she walked away, leaving Ethan standing there, his chest hollow and aching.

Ethan's jaw tightened as he turned back to Jeff. "You're making a mistake." Before Jeff could respond, Ethan's eyes darkened, his powers igniting as he wiped the memory of their conversation clean from the mayor's mind.

He left the room in a blur, running after Nora. He couldn't lose her—not like this.

He caught up with her just outside, grabbing her arm gently but firmly. "Nora, wait. Please."

She pulled away from his grasp, her voice cold and steady. "Let me go, Ethan. Let. Me. Go."

Reluctantly, he released her, but the desperation in his chest refused to let her leave. He tried to use his powers, to manipulate her emotions, but something was wrong. They weren't working. Nora remained unaffected, her eyes still blazing with fury and betrayal.

"Why did you do this?" Her voice cracked, a mixture of anger and heartbreak. Her face flushed with disbelief as she waited for an answer.

Ethan's throat tightened. "I didn't mean for it to happen," he began, his voice thick with regret. "It was a mistake, Nora. I'm so sorry. Baby, please-"

He dropped to his knees in front of her, his hands trembling. "Punish me, do whatever you want. Just- don't leave me."

For a moment, her expression softened. Then, she smiled—a bitter, almost mocking smile. "It's not going to be that easy, Ethan."

With that, she turned and walked away, her steps steady and determined. Ethan scrambled to his feet, following her, begging her to stay. But his words fell on deaf ears.

Days blurred together. Ethan shut himself off from the world, drowning in guilt and sorrow. Ava tried to contact him, but he couldn't bring himself to answer. He ignored her calls, his mind consumed by thoughts of Nora.

But one day, the knocks on his door shattered his isolation. When he opened it, Ava stood there, her face pale and full of fear.

"Ava? What are you doing here?" Ethan asked, startled by her sudden appearance.

"Is Nora home?" Her voice trembled, her eyes darting around nervously.

Ethan shook his head. "No, she's not here. Why? What's going on?"

Without waiting for an invitation, Ava pushed past him and into the apartment. She spun around to face him, her body trembling with fear before she broke down into sobs.

"Jeff- he's going to kill me, Ethan!" she cried, collapsing into his arms.

Ethan held her for a moment, trying to calm her, but his mind was racing. "You need to stand up to him, Ava. You can't let him control you like this."

"I can't," she sobbed harder, clutching his shirt. "I'm too scared."

Ethan sighed, pulling away from her. "If you won't stand up for yourself, then I can't help you."

Ava's sobs quieted, her voice barely a whisper as she looked up at him. "I'm pregnant, Ethan."

The words hit him like a freight train. "What?" His voice came out in a breathless whisper, disbelief coursing through him.

"I'm pregnant with your child," she repeated, tears streaming down her face. "And Jeff- he's going to kill me. He'll kill our baby too."

Ethan felt his world spin. He had never expected this— never imagined being in such a position. But one thing was clear: he wouldn't let Jeff lay a hand on Ava or their child.

He made the hard decision to send Ava away, out of the country, somewhere safe. As they drove toward the airport, the car was filled with a tense silence. Ava sat quietly beside him, her hands resting on her stomach. But just before they reached their destination, she spoke again.

"Nora isn't your girlfriend, Ethan," Ava said softly, her voice carrying an air of finality.

He frowned, glancing at her briefly. "What are you talking about?"

"She's been using you, manipulating your lost memories," Ava continued, her voice steady. She pulled out her phone and showed him a picture—one of her and Ethan together, looking happy, in love. But Ethan didn't remember it at all.

His grip tightened on the steering wheel, confusion flooding his mind. "What do you mean?"

Ava took a shaky breath. "You were mine, Ethan. We were together before they killed you."

Ethan's heart pounded in his chest, his head throbbing as fragments of memories he couldn't grasp flickered at the edges of his consciousness. He pulled the car over to the side of the road, unable to keep driving. "Killed me? What are you talking about?"

"They didn't just erase your memory," Ava whispered, tears welling in her eyes. "They killed you- and then brought you back. And now they're using you for their own purposes. Nora, Jeff- they've been controlling you."

Ethan stared at her, his mind reeling. None of it made sense, and yet, something deep inside him knew she was telling the truth. He looked down at the picture on her phone again, his heart twisting with both fear and anger.

Who was she? Who was Nora?

5

CHAPTER 5

Nora stood at the airport terminal, her eyes darting anxiously toward the arriving cars. Beside her was Jeffrey Coopland, flanked by his guards, their presence suffocating, their expressions hard. Tension hung heavy in the air as they waited for Ethan's arrival.

"Jeff, I've done my part. I brought Ava to you," Nora said, her voice tight. "Now leave Ethan out of this. You promised."

Jeffrey turned to her, his face dark with fury. He grabbed her by the chin, his fingers digging cruelly into her skin. "Promised? You said Ethan would never interfere in my life again," he hissed through clenched teeth. "So why the hell is he back?"

Nora's eyes bore into his, unflinching despite the pain. She knew he was seconds away from doing something rash, but she kept her composure—for Ethan's sake. "Maybe you should've kept a better eye on Ava instead of letting her slip away," she snapped, the anger in her voice thinly veiled.

A muscle in Jeffrey's jaw twitched, but before he could respond, one of the guards spoke up. "Mayor, they're here."

Nora's heart pounded in her chest as the group moved swiftly toward the car. Ethan's car. He was there, standing by his door, the cold steel of a gun pressed against him by one of Jeffrey's men.

Ethan's eyes immediately locked on Nora, confusion and betrayal swirling in their depths. "Nora, who the hell are you?" he demanded, his voice a mixture of anger and disbelief. The woman he thought was his girlfriend now felt like a stranger—a puppet in someone else's game.

Nora let out a chilling laugh, one that didn't reach her eyes. "Who am I?" she mocked. "You're trusting her? That bitch who cheated on her husband?"

Ava, now held captive by one of Jeffrey's guards, screamed in defiance, struggling against their hold. "You're evil! Don't trust them, Ethan! They'll kill you again!"

Ethan's gaze flicked between the two women, the weight of everything crashing down on him. Who could he believe? The lines between ally and enemy blurred in his mind. The Mayor gave a nod, and Ava was thrown into the back of his car, the door slamming shut with a finality that rang in Ethan's ears.

"Let's go home," Nora whispered, stepping toward Ethan and reaching for his hand. But the moment her fingers brushed his skin, he recoiled, shaking her off.

His voice was low, filled with disgust. "I don't know you."

Nora's eyes widened in disbelief, but then a cold, possessive rage flared within her. "What do you mean?" she snarled, stepping closer, her voice venomous. "I'm your girlfriend"

Ethan stood tall, finally seeing her for who she truly was. "No, you're not," he said quietly but firmly, the finality in his words cutting through the tension. "I have to save Ava."

Without waiting for a response, he turned and sprinted after the Mayor's car, his heart racing. But deep down, something told him he was already too late. He rounded the corner, only to find the car parked on the side of the road, Ava's lifeless body slumped over in the backseat, blood staining the seats.

"No- no- no" The word came out in a choked whisper, his legs giving out beneath him as he stumbled toward the scene. "Ava-"

Jeffrey stood off to the side, his expression cold and indifferent. "She killed herself," he said, the lie so thin it barely masked the truth. "She did it herself."

Ethan's heart shattered, a roar of grief and rage ripping through his chest. His child, Ava— gone, just like that. The pain twisted into something darker, something more primal.

Without hesitation, Ethan lunged at the guards. His body moved with the fury of a man with nothing left to lose. One by one, they fell beneath his relentless assault, each blow more lethal than the last. Bones cracked, blood sprayed, and soon, all that remained was the broken silence of the aftermath.

By the time the police arrived, it was a massacre. Ethan stood amidst the carnage, bloodied and breathing heavily, but his rage still burned hot in his veins. And then his eyes fell on Jeffrey.

The Mayor stood frozen, his hands raised in surrender, but there was no fear in his eyes— just arrogance. As if even now, he believed himself untouchable. "You think you've won, Ethan?" Jeffrey sneered. "You're nothing. I'll get you killed again."

Ethan's fists clenched, his vision narrowing as he stalked toward Jeffrey, looming over him. "Count your days Jeff," Ethan said, his voice dangerously calm, "You're the one at my mercy."

Jeffrey smirked, but there was a flicker of doubt in his eyes. "You can't kill me."

"No," Ethan said, crouching down so he was eye level with him. His voice dropped to a whisper, dripping with menace. "But I'll make sure you live in fear every day for the rest of your life. And when I'm done with you, you'll wish you had died today."

The Mayor's smirk faltered as Ethan stood, wiping the blood from his hands. The police moved in, taking control of the scene, but Ethan barely noticed. His mind was already miles away, consumed by thoughts of revenge and justice.

As he walked away, leaving Jeffrey and the wreckage behind, Ethan knew one thing for certain: this wasn't over. Not by a long shot. They had taken everything from him.

Now, it was his turn.

6

CHAPTER 6

Ethan sat in the cold, dimly lit cell, his hands shackled, his body a mixture of bruises and scars from the violent confrontation that had ended in bloodshed.

His thoughts were a hurricane of rage and grief, swirling endlessly around the memory of Ava's lifeless body. The weight of losing his child crushed him, but beneath the despair, a singular, dark purpose had taken root—revenge. He would make every single person responsible for Ava's death pay, starting with Jeffrey, and perhaps, eventually- Nora.

For now, though, all he could do was wait.

Nora came every day. Like clockwork. She would saunter into the visitation room, a smile stretched across her face, her eyes glowing with a possessive madness. Her voice, sickly sweet, grated against his nerves every time she spoke. She has arranged with the gaurds to provide him his necessity - blood.

"You belong to me, Ethan. No matter what you do or say. You're mine, and nothing will change that."

Ethan clenched his fists, jaw tight, barely containing the seething anger that threatened to explode every time she sat across from him. He warned her every day, just as calmly and coldly as the day before. "I will make you pay for what you've done, Nora. For what you've taken from me. When I get out, you and everyone else involved in Ava's death—they'll all suffer. I swear it."

But Nora's response was always the same. She laughed, a sound so hollow and manic that it crawled under his skin. She didn't care about his threats. She didn't care about his vengeance. In her twisted mind, Ethan was hers, and no amount of hatred or fury could change that.

"Ava, for her you're willing to ruin your life. You never even loved her?" Her voice carried a delusion that sickened him.

Every word out of her mouth was like poison, dripping into his already fractured mind. But he endured. Every day that passed, every one of her visits, only fueled his determination. He would escape, and when he did, she would be the first to feel his wrath.

Days bled into weeks, and weeks into months. Ethan waited, silently plotting his escape, his mind working tirelessly behind the walls of his cell. He was patient. He knew his time would come.

And then, it did.

On a stormy night, amidst the chaos of a prison riot, Ethan saw his chance. The guards were distracted, shouts echoing through the halls as inmates fought, fires breaking out in various cells. In the midst of the bedlam, Ethan slipped out, his movements quick and calculated.

He overpowered a guard, taking the man's keys and slipping unnoticed into the shadows of the prison's labyrinthine corridors. When the alarms finally blared, he was long gone.

By the time anyone realized what had happened, Ethan was already miles away, heading straight for Nora.

He found her alone, as he knew he would. The town was quiet, everyone in a frenzy over the prison break, and she had let her guard down. Ethan's grip tightened around her wrist as he yanked her from her home, his eyes blazing with cold fury.

"You're coming with me," he growled, dragging her toward the car.

Nora, instead of fighting, laughed, a sickening sound. "I knew you'd come for me. You can't resist me, can you?" Her voice was thick with delusion, her eyes wide with twisted affection.

Ethan said nothing. His silence was more terrifying than any threat he could have uttered. He wasn't taking her because he wanted her. He was taking her because she was part of his plan. A pawn in the greater game of his revenge. He was going to make her regret every second of her life.

They drove for hours, the car speeding through desolate roads until they reached the middle of nowhere—an abandoned cabin surrounded by acres of tall, wild grass. No one would find them here. It was the perfect hiding place. The perfect place to break her. And to make her watch as he fulfilled his vengeance.

Ethan threw Nora into the cabin, the door slamming behind them. She hit the floor but quickly scrambled to her feet, her eyes gleaming with excitement instead of fear.

"What is this place?" she asked, a smile tugging at her lips. "Are you planning to kill me here?"

Ethan stalked toward her, his body towering over hers, his expression cold and devoid of emotion. "This is where it ends, Nora," he said, his voice low and dangerous. "You took everything from me. Now, I'll take everything from you."

Nora's smile faltered, but only for a second. She stepped closer to him, her fingers brushing against his chest. "You can't hurt me, Ethan. I know you. You can't kill me?"

Ethan's hand shot out, gripping her chin with brutal force. He brought her face close to his, his breath hot against her skin as he whispered, "You don't know anything about me."

Her eyes flickered with uncertainty, but she didn't pull away. She never did. She was too obsessed, too lost in her own delusions to see the storm brewing in Ethan's eyes.

Days passed, each one darker than the last. Ethan kept her bound, trapped in the cabin, forcing her to endure the isolation and fear she had forced upon him. He never laid a hand on her, never harmed her physically. But the psychological torment was worse. He would disappear for hours, leaving her alone, only to return and ignore her existence entirely. He let her fear and madness eat away at her, just as she had tried to break him.

Nora, once confident and deranged with her obsession, began to unravel. The cabin, the isolation, Ethan's cold indifference—it all chipped away at her manic façade.

"Let me go Ethan." Her demand turned to requests, then cries and wails.

And then, one night, as the wind howled outside, Nora finally broke. She collapsed onto the floor, her sobs filling the small cabin. "Please, Ethan- don't leave me. I need you. I love you."

Ethan stood over her, his gaze hard, unfeeling. He crouched down, his voice a low growl. "This isn't love, Nora. This is an obsession. And it ends now."

Revenge was close— he could taste it. And when it came, no one, not even Nora, would escape

7

CHAPTER 7

The room was dimly lit, shadows dancing across the walls of the secluded cabin. The distant cries of the wind howled outside as if the world itself mourned the sins committed within. Ethan leaned against the wooden wall, his eyes fixed on Nora, bound to the chair in front of him.

She wasn't the Nora he remembered. Or maybe she was, and he had just been blind to it all along. Her eyes gleamed with an eerie calmness, the corner of her lips twitching into what looked like the faintest smile.

"Waiting for something?" she asked, her voice cold and almost mocking. She had barely flinched when he dragged her in here, tied her up, and starved her for days.

The cruelty he had subjected her to didn't break her; instead, it seemed to reveal something even darker within her.

Ethan narrowed his eyes, pacing slowly around the room. "You'll crack," he said evenly. "It's only a matter of time."

Nora chuckled softly, tilting her head to the side as she looked at him. "You think I'm afraid of you, Ethan?" Her voice was steady, devoid of the pleading he'd been expecting. "We're the same, you and I. The only difference is you're still pretending you're not a monster."

He stopped pacing, turning to face her. The darkness in his eyes flickered with anger. "Don't compare me to you. I'm nothing like you."

"Oh, really?" she replied, her voice dripping with sarcasm. "You're here, torturing me, seeking revenge—just like I would do. We're both liars. Both killers."

Ethan's jaw tightened. He wanted her to scream, to beg for mercy, but this wasn't the reaction he had expected. Nora's calmness unnerved him, her defiance throwing him off balance. He had underestimated her. She wasn't the desperate, lovesick woman he thought she'd be. She was something else entirely—something far more dangerous.

He crouched down in front of her, grabbing her by the chin and forcing her to meet his gaze. "You're going to pay for what you did. Ava didn't deserve any of this. Our child—my child—didn't deserve this."

Nora's eyes bore into his, unblinking. "And neither did I," she whispered, her voice venomous. "But that's life, Ethan. People like us- we take what we want, we destroy what gets in our way. Ava was just collateral damage. You would have seen that eventually, if you hadn't been so blinded by your pathetic little fantasy of being the hero."

His grip tightened on her chin, his knuckles white. "You don't get to talk about her."

"Why not?" she sneered, her smile widening. "She's dead, Ethan. Dead because of you. Because you couldn't protect her."

He shoved her back, rising to his feet, his breathing labored with rage. "Shut your mouth," he warned, his voice dangerously low.

But Nora only laughed, the sound sending a chill down his spine. "You're weak," she said. "You've always been weak. That's why I played you so easily. You wanted to believe I was something else, something good. But deep down, you knew, didn't you? You knew what I was capable of."

Ethan's hands clenched into fists, his nails digging into his palms. The memories of their time together flashed through his mind—the lies, the manipulation. She had deceived him, made him believe that she loved him. And all the while, she had been plotting against him.

"You think you're so clever," he said, his voice shaking with barely contained fury. "But you're nothing. Jeff's going to pay for what he did, and so will you."

Nora raised an eyebrow, unfazed by his threat. "Jeff?" She let out a small, humorless laugh. "You don't know, what he's capable of!"

Ethan's heart pounded in his chest. He leaned in close, his face inches from hers. "Then why don't you enlighten me?"

Nora's eyes sparkled with twisted amusement. "I don't need to. You'll figure it out soon enough."

8

CHAPTER 8

Ethan stepped away from her, grabbing a piece of raw meat from the cooler in the corner. He threw it at her feet, the slab of flesh hitting the ground with a sickening thud. Nora glanced down at it, her expression unreadable.

"You hungry?" Ethan asked, his voice cold. "You've been begging for food for days. Go on. Eat."

Nora raised an eyebrow, her lips curling into a smirk. "What is this? Some kind of test?"

He said nothing, only watching as she eyed the meat suspiciously. After a long pause, she leaned forward, picking up the slab with her bound hands. She examined it closely before taking a small bite.

Ethan watched, waiting for the moment she realized the truth.

As she chewed, her face remained expressionless. She swallowed, looking up at him with a bored sigh.

"Human flesh." Ethan lied, eyeing Nora as her expression changed to utter horror.

Nora's eyes widened in surprise. "what the fuck-" she spit it out and threw up at that point.

"You're sick," she replied, dropping the meat back onto the floor. "What do you think, this would make me go frenzy? Is this all you got?"

Ethan's hands shook as anger surged through him. He wanted her to break, to crumble beneath the weight of his revenge. But instead, she stared back at him, unafraid and unfazed.

"You're already crazy," he spat, his voice filled with rage.

"And you're a hypocrite," Nora shot back, her eyes gleaming with malice. "You're no better than me. You've killed. You've tortured. You're standing here, trying to make me suffer for the same things you're guilty of."

"I'm doing this for Ava!" Ethan shouted, his voice echoing through the cabin.

"No," Nora said calmly. "You're doing this because you want to. Because deep down, this is who you are. A monster. Just like me."

He grabbed her by the throat, his fingers digging into her skin as he lifted her slightly off the chair. "I'm not like you," he growled, his face inches from hers. "I'm nothing like you."

Nora's lips curled into a sinister smile, even as his grip tightened around her neck. "Keep telling yourself that, Ethan. Maybe one day you'll believe it."

He released her suddenly, letting her fall back into the chair, gasping for air. He turned away, pacing the room again, his mind racing. She was getting to him, and he hated it. He need-ed to break her, to make her suffer as he had suffered.

But no matter what he did, she remained unbroken.

Later that night, Ethan dragged Nora into the bathroom, her body limp as he threw her into the cold, porcelain tub. She lay there, staring up at the ceiling, her breathing shallow but steady.

He turned on the faucet, letting the water fill the tub slowly. It was freezing, but Nora didn't flinch. She simply watched him, her eyes never leaving his face.

"You're not going to win," he said, his voice barely above a whisper as the water reached her waist. "I already have," she replied, her voice soft but filled with conviction.

Ethan's rage boiled over. He grabbed her by the hair, shoving her face beneath the water. Her body thrashed violently, but he held her down, watching the bubbles rise to the surface as she struggled for air.

Just as her movements began to slow, he pulled her back up, letting her gasp and sputter for breath. But there was no fear in her eyes. Only defiance.

"You think this scares me?" she asked, her voice hoarse but unwavering. "You'll never break me, Ethan. I'm stronger than you'll ever be."

He shoved her under again, holding her down longer this time, his hands steady as she kicked and struggled. But even as she drowned, her eyes never lost that glint of defiance, that smug assurance that she would survive this.

And that was what terrified him the most.

9

CHAPTER 9

The air outside the cabin was dense with the weight of impending storm clouds, and the only sounds breaking the silence were the howling wind and the rustling of the tall grass around the cabin.

Nora's hands trembled as she worked her wrists free from the ropes that had bound her for days. Her muscles ached from the strain, her body weak from starvation, but her mind was sharp, fueled by a dangerous mixture of determination and rage.

She knew she had only a small window of time. Ethan had gone out, likely in search of his next victim or plotting his eventual attack on Jeff. Nora's every movement was calculated. She needed to get out. Now.

Finally, the ropes gave way, and she bolted up from the chair. Her body screamed in protest, but she ignored the pain. Blood trickled down her wrists where the ropes had cut into her skin, but there was no time to worry about that. She stumbled toward the cabin door, glancing over her shoulder at the dark interior, half-expecting Ethan to burst in at any moment.

Her hand hovered over the doorknob, heart pounding so hard she thought it might explode from her chest. She turned the knob slowly, silently, and slipped out into the open air.

The world outside the cabin was eerily quiet, a vast stretch of desolation—acres of tall grass waving in the wind, the ground uneven and treacherous beneath her bare feet. But freedom was in sight. The sky loomed heavy with the threat of rain, and for the first time in days, Nora felt the sting of hope. She ran, her bare feet cutting on the jagged rocks, but she pushed herself forward, ignoring the searing pain shooting up her legs.

The grass whipped at her as she sprinted toward the edge of the property. But as she approached, a sinking realization gripped her. A barbed wire fence surrounded the perimeter, razor-sharp and glinting under the gray sky. She came to a halt, panting, eyes wide in desperation. There was no way over it without suffering serious injury.

Nora didn't care. The pain would be worth it. She approached the fence, stretching her arms up to grab hold of the wire, ready to pull herself over. Blood began to bead along her hands as the barbs dug into her skin, slicing her flesh open. She winced but didn't let go, trying to lift herself higher, inch by inch.

Suddenly, she heard the distant crunch of footsteps behind her. "No, no, no- " she whispered, panic surging through her. She didn't dare look back, knowing who it would be. Ethan. He was back, and she wasn't free—not yet.

Before she could hoist herself fully over the fence, a hand—strong, brutal—wrapped around her ankle, yanking her down with such force that she slammed into the ground. She screamed, her voice tearing through the air as her body was dragged backward, the sharp barbs raking against her legs, leaving deep gashes.

Ethan's grip tightened around her ankle as he dragged her through the tall grass, her fingers clawing at the dirt, trying in vain to find something to hold on to. The agony from her injuries blurred with the terror coursing through her veins. He didn't say a word, but the fury in his silence was deafening.

"Let go of me!" she screamed, kicking out with her free leg. But Ethan was relentless, his strength overpowering hers as he dragged her closer and closer to the cabin.

When they reached the cabin's threshold, he finally released her, her body limp and bloodied on the ground. She gasped for air, coughing, her chest heaving as she scrambled to sit up. But Ethan was there, towering over her, his face shadowed with barely contained rage.

"You thought you could leave?" His voice was cold, terrifyingly calm, as he looked down at her.

Nora spat blood onto the ground, defiant despite the agony wracking her body. "I'm not your prisoner," she hissed. "You'll never own me."

Ethan's expression darkened, his jaw clenching as he knelt beside her. His hand shot out, grabbing her face in a vice-like grip, forcing her to look into his eyes. "You're mine, Nora. You were always mine." His words were venomous, each syllable dripping with a twisted sense of possession.

Nora's eyes blazed with fury, refusing to give him the satisfaction of fear. "You don't own anything. Not me, not Ava, and definitely not your revenge. You're just a weak man, chasing ghosts."

Ethan's nostrils flared, and for a moment, Nora thought he might kill her right there. But instead, he let go of her face and grabbed her by the hair, yanking her to her feet. She stumbled, her legs barely able to hold her weight, but she didn't beg. She wouldn't give him that.

He dragged her back into the cabin, her body weak, barely able to resist. But her mind was still sharp, her eyes watching every movement, searching for a weakness in his madness. He slammed the door behind them, the air inside thick with tension.

"You think this is a game?" he growled, throwing her back into the chair where she had spent countless days tied up, starved, humiliated.Nora glared at him, blood dripping down her face from a gash on her forehead. "I know it is. And you're losing."

Ethan's eyes darkened with fury, but there was something else in his gaze—uncertainty. He expected her to be terrified, broken, but she wasn't. And it unnerved him.

He moved toward her again, rope in hand, his knuckles white from how tightly he was gripping it. "I'll make you wish you never tried to leave," he threatened, his voice low and dangerous.

Nora's lips twisted into a smile, even through the pain. "You'll have to do better than that, Ethan."

With a growl, he tied her down once more, tightening the knots so brutally that her wrists turned purple. But through it all, Nora didn't scream. She didn't cry. She only stared at him, that same maddening smile playing on her lips, as if daring him to do his worst.

As Ethan stood over her, his breath ragged from anger, he realized something chilling.

Nora wasn't afraid of him. She never had been.

And that was what terrified him most of all.

10

CHAPTER 10

Ethan stood over Nora, his chest rising and falling rapidly, anger coursing through his veins.

He had caught her again. She'd tried to escape, thought she could defy him. His hands twitched with the urge to punish her, to remind her exactly who she belonged to. The barred wire outside had torn at her skin, but her resolve had been clear—she would risk everything to get away from him. That realization only made his anger grow stronger.

With one swift motion, he yanked her up by her wrists, the ropes around them barely loosening from her earlier struggle. Nora's breath was heavy, chest rising and falling as she stared back at him with defiance, her lips pressed into a hard line. Even now, after everything, she wasn't afraid of him. That defiance lit something dark inside Ethan, something more dangerous than the rage.

Without a word, he crashed his lips against hers, gripping her by the back of her neck as if forcing her to bend to his will.

His kiss was hard, unforgiving, filled with the anger he hadn't yet expressed. Nora fought against him, twisting her body to pull away, but it only made him hold on tighter. He kissed her as if punishing her, teeth grazing her lips roughly.

"You're mine," he growled between kisses, his voice low and dangerous, dripping with possessiveness.

His hands roamed down her body, clawing at the fabric of her shirt, tearing it open with a single rough pull. Her bare skin was exposed to the cold air of the cabin, and still, she resisted, fighting him even as her body trembled from exhaustion.

Ethan's hands were everywhere—rough, demanding—his fingers digging into her flesh as if trying to mold her into submission. He dragged her closer, and when she tried to push him away, he gripped her tighter, his fingers digging into her skin, leaving bruises behind.

"Stop!" Nora screamed, her voice raw and hoarse. But Ethan wasn't listening. The need to break her, to make her his in every way, drowned out her pleas.

It wasn't until he forced her down, his body heavy on top of hers, that the truth hit him—she was still untouched. A virgin. The realization stunned him, momentarily freezing his movements. Nora, with all her strength, her defiance, had never been with anyone else. She had never let anyone touch her like this.

But then, something twisted in his mind. Instead of stopping, it fueled him. The sick need to take what no one else had. To claim her as his, fully and completely.

Nora tried to resist, her body thrashing beneath him, but it was useless. She was too tired, too worn from the days of captivity. Ethan's strength overpowered her as he forced himself inside, a painful cry escaping her lips. She clenched her fists, digging her nails into his back, but it only seemed to encourage him. His pace was relentless, and every movement was filled with a violent need to dominate.

Tears streamed down her face, but not once did she beg him to stop. She hated him. She hated him with every fiber of her being, and yet- her body eventually gave in, her strength waning as his unrelenting assault continued.

When it was finally over, Ethan rolled off her, breathing heavily, his chest rising and falling. He didn't look at her at first, almost as if avoiding her gaze. Nora lay still, trembling, her mind numb to what had just happened. She had fought so hard, and yet, in the end, it hadn't mattered.

Ethan stood, his back to her as he dressed himself, his body shaking with an emotion even he couldn't fully understand. Guilt, satisfaction, possessiveness—it all mixed into something dark and complicated. He couldn't bring himself to feel remorse, not truly. She was his now, in every sense of the word.

The next morning, Ethan moved through the cabin with eerie calm. He filled the bathtub with cold water and carried Nora to it, her body limp and unresponsive. He lowered her into the water, her skin prickling from the icy touch. As he bathed her, his hands were surprisingly gentle, as if this act of washing away the remnants of the night was somehow meant to soothe her.

Nora didn't resist this time. She was too exhausted, too broken from the events of the previous night. Her mind was far away, detached from her body, as Ethan's hands moved over her, cleaning the bruises, the dried blood, and sweat from her skin.

"You're mine now," he whispered softly, his lips brushing against her ear as he rinsed her hair. "You'll always be mine- my doll."

The words sent a shiver down Nora's spine. Doll. That's what she had become to him—something to own, to control. Ethan smiled down at her, his touch disturbingly tender as he lifted her out of the tub and dried her off with a towel. He dressed her in a clean white shirt, one of his, and led her to the small kitchen.

The smell of food wafted through the air—eggs, toast, and bacon sizzling on the stove. It was almost surreal, the way he moved around the kitchen as if they were a normal couple. Nora sat at the table, her wrists still raw from the ropes, her body aching, and yet- she ate. The hunger gnawing at her stomach was too much to resist, and despite everything, she picked up the fork and forced herself to eat.

Ethan watched her closely, his eyes dark with an emotion she couldn't quite read. "Eat, doll," he urged softly, pushing a plate of food toward her. "You need your strength. To live."

Nora's hand trembled as she picked up a piece of toast, her mind still swimming from the horrors of the night before. But she ate. Slowly, methodically, she ate, knowing that her survival depended on it.When she had finished, Ethan stood up and walked over to her, kneeling down beside her chair. He tilted her chin up, forcing her to look into his eyes.

"You belong to me now," he whispered, his voice low and commanding. "Never try to escape again, or I will make you suffer. More than you can imagine."

Nora stared back at him, her eyes hollow but still filled with a spark of resistance. She didn't respond, but Ethan's grip on her chin tightened, his smile widening as he leaned in closer.

"You'll learn," he said softly, almost lovingly. "You'll learn that you're mine. Forever."

11

CHAPTER 11

The night was dark, and the air was thick with tension. Ethan knew this was the moment he had been waiting for, the moment to finally close the chapter on Jeffrey.

The police had stopped searching for him and Nora, and with no one left on his tail, it was time for revenge. His every movement was calculated, and his heart pounded with a rhythm that matched the storm that brewed in the sky above.

Nora sat in the cabin, cuffed and locked up, her defiant gaze following him as he prepared to leave. "Don't even think about trying to escape this time," Ethan warned, his voice cold and devoid of emotion as he locked the doors. He knew she wouldn't be able to get far, not with the chains around her wrists and the reinforced locks he'd secured.

He was ready-his anger fueling every step. With his unnatural speed, Ethan darted through the darkened countryside, his eyes set on one destination: Jeffrey Coopland.

He had followed Jeffrey closely for days, learning his routine, his every move. Tonight, Jeffrey would be alone. No guards, no protection. Just him and Ethan, and the final reckoning.

The day passed in a haze for Ethan, every minute only building the anticipation of what he would do when he finally got his hands on the man responsible for everything-Ava's death, his child's death. The memories of it were burned into his mind, festering like an open wound that could only be healed with blood.By nightfall, Ethan stood in the shadows, watching Jeffrey's mansion from the darkness.

The house was quiet, the lights dimmed, signaling that his prey had retired for the night. His heart raced with a mixture of exhilaration and rage as he made his way inside, his movements silent, his presence unnoticed.

He crept up the stairs, every step taking him closer to Jeffrey's room. His breathing was steady, his eyes locked on the door ahead. Inside, Jeffrey lay asleep, completely unaware that the monster he had created was standing just a few feet away.

Ethan opened the door with a slow, deliberate creak, stepping inside without making a sound. Jeffrey stirred slightly but didn't wake-his guard lowered in the presumed safety of his own home. Ethan hovered over him, his shadow stretching long across the bed.

Finally, Jeffrey's eyes fluttered open, meeting the darkness before him. He blinked in confusion, his mind still groggy from sleep. Then, as recognition dawned, his face twisted in horror. "E-Ethan?" he stammered, trying to sit up. But Ethan was too quick.

Grabbing him by the throat, Ethan shoved him back down onto the bed, his grip tightening until Jeffrey gasped for air. "You remember me, don't you?" Ethan's voice was low, a dangerous growl, his eyes glowing with murderous intent. "You thought you could get away with everything you did?"

Jeffrey's hands clawed at Ethan's arm, his face turning red as he struggled to breathe. "P-please-" he managed to choke out, his eyes wide with fear.

Ethan leaned in closer, his face inches from Jeffrey's, his voice a deadly whisper. "I told you I'd make you pay, didn't I? For Ava. For my child. You took everything from me." His grip tightened, and Jeffrey's face contorted in pain, his body shaking with fear.

Tears filled Jeffrey's eyes as he whimpered, "I'll give you anything, anything you want. Just don't kill me."

Ethan's eyes gleamed with dark satisfaction. This was what he had wanted-to see the mighty Jeffrey Coopland reduced to a sniveling, broken man, begging for his life. "I don't want anything from you," Ethan said coldly. "Except your death."

With one swift motion, Ethan twisted Jeffrey's neck, the sickening crack echoing through the room as his body went limp. The silence that followed was deafening. Jeffrey's lifeless eyes stared up at the ceiling, the last remnants of life extinguished by Ethan's hand.

It was done. The man who had caused so much destruction was dead.Ethan stood there for a moment, staring down at the body, the rush of satisfaction filling him momentarily. But it wasn't enough. The darkness inside him hadn't been sated.

He left the mansion as quietly as he had entered, his clothes drenched in blood and rain as the storm outside finally broke. The rain pelted down on him, washing away some of the blood but not the violence that still clung to him.

When Ethan returned to the cabin, he was soaked through, his hair plastered to his forehead, his eyes dark and wild. Blood still stained his hands and his clothes, mixing with the rain as he stepped inside. Nora looked up from her place on the floor, her wrists raw from the cuffs. But for the first time, her defiance faltered.

There was something different about him now. Something darker. More monstrous. The man who had left her earlier that night had returned as something else entirely-a beast, drenched in blood and revenge.

Ethan's gaze met Nora's, and for the first time since she had been taken, she felt something stir inside her that she hadn't expected: fear. The kind of fear that made her stomach turn, her pulse quicken. She had known Ethan was dangerous, but this- this was different.His eyes locked on hers, and she saw no remorse, no hesitation-only the cold, hard satisfaction of a man who had tasted blood and wanted more.

"I told you what would happen," he said, his voice low and rough as he stepped closer to her. His presence was suffocating, the smell of rain and blood heavy in the air. "Jeffrey is dead. And now-"

Nora swallowed hard, her throat dry as she watched him approach. She tried to steel herself, to hold onto the strength she had clung to for so long. But it was slipping, fading under the weight of the monster that stood before her.

"Now, It's your turn."

He knelt down in front of her, his hand reaching out to brush a strand of wet hair from her face. The touch was deceptively gentle, but she could feel the violence simmering beneath the surface. Nora wanted to pull away, to fight back, but for the first time, she wasn't sure if she could. Ethan had changed, and the man she had once toyed with, manipulated, was gone.

In his place was something far more dangerous. Something she wasn't sure she could survive.

"You felt it, didn't you?" Ethan's voice was soft, almost a whisper. "That fear. You thought you could escape me, but now you know- there's no getting away."

Nora's heart pounded in her chest, her mind racing as she tried to think of something- anything-to break the spell he had over her. But all she could do was stare into those dark, bloodshot eyes and realize the truth. The real monster had finally revealed itself. And there was no escape.

12

CHAPTER 12

Ethan stood before Nora, drenched in rain and blood, his eyes locked on hers with an intensity that sent a chill down her spine. There was something about the way he looked at her now-something far more primal and dangerous than anything she had seen before. The air between them crackled with tension, thick and suffocating.

"Are you scared?" Ethan's voice was low, almost a growl as he took a step closer. "Because you should be, doll."

Nora's heart raced, but she kept her expression neutral, refusing to show him the fear that twisted in her gut. Her mind raced, searching for any escape from the monster that now stood before her. But she knew there was none. Ethan had her trapped-physically and mentally.

He reached out, his hand cupping her chin, tilting her face up toward him. "You've always been so defiant, haven't you?" His thumb grazed her lower lip as he leaned closer, his breath hot against her skin. "But you know, deep down, you belong to me."

Nora's breath caught in her throat, her lips parting slightly as his thumb lingered there. She didn't want to give him the satisfaction of knowing how much his presence affected her, but her body betrayed her. Her pulse quickened, heat flooding through her as he stared down at her, his gaze dark and possessive.

Ethan's lips crashed against hers suddenly, and despite the terror that gripped her, there was a spark of something else-something she couldn't deny. She kissed him back, her hands gripping his soaked shirt, pulling him closer even as her mind screamed at her to resist. His hands were rough, his kiss demanding, and there was no mistaking the raw power behind it.

He pushed her backward until her body collided with the wall, his hands gripping her waist, sliding under her shirt as he tore it away. Nora gasped, her mind spinning as she felt the heat of his touch, the overwhelming force of his desire.

"You're mine, Nora," Ethan murmured against her lips, his voice full of dark promise. "You always have been."

Nora's knees weakened as his lips trailed down her neck, and though every part of her mind screamed to resist, her body betrayed her once more. She felt the undeniable pull toward him, the raw connection that bound them in ways she couldn't understand. But this was different-Ethan had changed, and with him, so had the nature of what they shared.

She couldn't suppress the heat building between them, the way his touch ignited something dark and deep within her. And when he lifted her effortlessly into his arms and carried her to the bed, she didn't fight him.

Nora's body trembled as Ethan's hands roamed over her, his touch possessive and unrelenting. The room spun as he undressed her, piece by piece, until she was completely exposed before him. She felt vulnerable, but there was a twisted part of her that reveled in it-the way he dominated her, the way he made her feel as though she was truly his.

But when the moment grew too intense, when her mind could no longer reconcile the rush of desire with the fear that gnawed at her, Nora pushed him away and stumbled into the bathroom, slamming the door behind her.

Her breath came in ragged gasps as she leaned against the sink, her reflection in the mirror staring back at her-a mix of fear, confusion, and an undeniable hunger she couldn't understand. She didn't want to feel this way, didn't want to be drawn to him. But Ethan had unlocked something inside her, something primal and consuming.

Before she could collect her thoughts, the door burst open. Ethan stood in the doorway, his eyes wild and dark, filled with something raw and dangerous. He didn't say a word as he stepped inside, shutting the door behind him.

"Ethan-" Nora's voice trembled, but there was no time for words. He crossed the distance between them in an instant, his hands gripping her hips as he pulled her against him.

"Running won't save you," Ethan growled, his breath hot against her ear. "You can't escape me."

He kissed her again, harder this time, with a need that seemed to devour her whole. Nora's resolve crumbled as she gave in, her body responding to his with a ferocity that mirrored his own. His hands explored her, claiming every inch of her skin as he pinned her against the cold tile wall.

She didn't resist. She couldn't.His lips moved down her neck, across her collarbone, leaving a trail of fire in their wake. Nora's fingers tangled in his hair, pulling him closer, deeper, as their bodies collided with a force that shook her to her core.

Ethan's hands gripped her thighs, lifting her up as he pressed her against the wall, and in that moment, it was as though nothing else existed-just the heat of their connection, the raw intensity that consumed them both.

The rain outside pounded against the cabin, matching the rhythm of their bodies as Ethan made love to her with an intensity that bordered on brutal. Nora's mind was a blur, her body reacting instinctively to every touch, every movement. The fear she had felt moments ago was now overshadowed by something far darker-a need, a desire that ran deeper than she could have imagined.When it was over, and they lay tangled together in the aftermath, Nora's mind finally caught up with her. She stared at the ceiling, her breath coming in shallow gasps, her body trembling from the intensity of what had just happened.Ethan kissed her forehead softly, his voice a low whisper in the darkness. "You're mine now, Doll. Never forget that."

Nora's heart raced as the weight of his words settled over her. She had crossed a line, one she could never come back from. Ethan had claimed her, body and soul, and in that moment, she knew there was no escaping the monster she had become entangled with.

The next morning, Ethan woke first. He carried her to the bathroom, gently washing her as if nothing violent had happened between them. His touch was almost tender, his eyes watching her with a strange mixture of possession and admiration.As he bathed her, he whispered, "You're my Doll now. Don't ever try to run again." There was a warning in his tone, a promise of what would come if she ever defied him.

Nora remained silent, her mind still reeling from the events of the night before. She wasn't sure who she had become in that cabin, but one thing was clear: there was no going back now. Not from him. Not from this.

Ethan fed her breakfast, his demeanor oddly calm and caring as he made sure she ate every bite. But the underlying threat in his eyes was impossible to ignore.

"Try to leave again," Ethan said as he set the plate aside, "and you'll suffer in ways you can't imagine."Nora met his gaze, her heart pounding in her chest. She knew he meant every word.

13

CHAPTER 13

Nora had become a doll of her own creation, trapped in the twisted world that Ethan had built around them. Each day, he would care for her like she was his prized possession. He'd bathe her meticulously, run his hands through her hair, dress her in clothes that he chose, and then tie her back up as if she were nothing more than an object for him to control.Some days, he'd let her out into the yard, letting her feel the sun on her skin and the grass beneath her feet, but even then, she was never truly free. Ethan would cuff himself to her, ensuring that every step she took was tethered to him, a constant reminder of the chains that bound them together—physically and mentally.

Nora's mind had grown numb to the routine, her defiance worn down by the relentless cycle of control and submission. But deep down, the fire hadn't gone out completely. One day, as they stood in the yard, Ethan's grip on her chain as firm as ever, she couldn't help but ask the question that had been gnawing at her soul.

"How long do you plan to keep me like this, Ethan?" Her voice was calm, but beneath it lay a trace of exhaustion, a resignation to the nightmare that had become her life.

Ethan's lips curled into a mocking smile, his dark eyes glinting with amusement. "Until I'm bored," he replied nonchalantly. "Or until you die. Whichever comes first."

Nora's heart sank at his words, though she had expected nothing less. Her lips trembled as she asked the next question, the one that had been lingering in the back of her mind for days. "Then kill me already."

Her words were simple, but they struck Ethan like a whip. His mocking smile vanished in an instant, replaced by a dark fury that simmered beneath the surface. For a moment, silence stretched between them, thick and suffocating. Then, without warning, he grabbed her arm, dragging her back into the cabin with a force that made her stumble.

"You want to die, huh?" Ethan's voice was low, seething with anger. He slammed the door shut behind them, locking her inside the prison that had become their home.

Nora's heart pounded in her chest as she realized she had pushed him too far. Ethan's eyes were wild, the monster inside him fully unleashed now, and she knew what was coming.

Before she could say another word, he shoved her against the wall, his hands gripping her wrists so tightly that it hurt. "You think you can just ask for death and I'll give it to you? You think you can control when this ends?"

Nora's breath hitched, but she met his gaze, defiance flickering in her eyes even as fear twisted in her stomach. "I'm already dead," she whispered. "You killed me the day you took everything away."

That was all it took to push him over the edge. Ethan's fury ignited, and without another word, he dragged her to the bedroom. He threw her down onto the bed, his eyes dark with rage and desire, his control slipping further with every second.

"You want to die, Doll?" Ethan spat the words as he yanked at her clothes, tearing them away with no care for her protests. "I'll give you something worse than death."

Nora struggled beneath him, her body fighting instinctively even though her mind knew it was futile. Ethan's hands were everywhere—rough, demanding, punishing. He bound her wrists with the ropes that had become so familiar, tying her to the headboard as he leaned over her, his breath hot against her skin.

"You're mine," Ethan growled, his voice dripping with possession as he yanked her legs apart. "I'll make sure you never forget it."

He didn't waste time. His hands gripped her thighs, his movements forceful, bordering on brutal. Nora's resistance faltered as his dominance overwhelmed her, her body betraying her once more. She gasped as he entered her, her mind screaming for release from the torment, but her body responding to the raw, animalistic power of the moment.

Ethan's hands tightened around her wrists as he drove into her with a fury that bordered on madness. His pace was relentless, each thrust a reminder of the control he held over her, of the power he wielded in this twisted relationship. Nora's cries echoed through the room, a mixture of pain and unwanted pleasure as she struggled to keep herself from breaking completely.

But even in the midst of the brutal act, something inside her shifted. She wasn't just the broken doll he thought she was. There was a part of her that reveled in the darkness, in the intensity of the power he wielded over her. It was twisted, yes, but it was hers as much as it was his. Ethan had created this monster, and now she was becoming part of it.

When it was over, they were both breathless, drenched in sweat. Ethan collapsed beside her, his chest rising and falling rapidly. He looked at her with a wild, almost manic glint in his eyes.

"You're mine, Doll," he whispered, his voice still rough from the exertion. "And you'll never escape me."

Nora's wrists ached from the bindings, her body bruised and exhausted, but there was a small part of her that smiled inwardly. He thought he had her completely, but he didn't realize that she had started to claim him too.

Ethan reached out and untied her wrists, his touch gentler now, almost apologetic. He pulled her into his arms, cradling her like she was fragile, like he hadn't just ravaged her moments before.

"I'll take care of you," he murmured against her hair. "You're mine. Forever."

Nora didn't respond. She simply lay there, her mind racing as she tried to make sense of what had just happened. Ethan may have thought he was in control, but she knew now that control was an illusion. They were both caught in the same dark web, tied together by their shared madness.

The next morning, Ethan bathed her, as he always did. His hands were gentle again, his demeanor calm and collected. He dressed her in a new outfit, one that he had chosen for her, and he fed her breakfast as if nothing had happened.

But there was something different now. Nora wasn't just a doll anymore. She was becoming something more, something darker, something that Ethan couldn't fully control.

As she ate the food he placed in front of her, she glanced at him, her eyes cold but calculating. He may have been the monster that dragged her into this nightmare, but she was learning to navigate the darkness.

14

— · —

CHAPTER 14

The air around the cabin grew tense when the police knocked on the door. Ethan's gaze locked with Nora's, a flicker of doubt crossing his eyes. "If they find me, it's over," he warned in a low growl, his voice laced with the promise of violence. "This could turn into a bloodbath if you betray me."

Nora remained calm, her mind spinning with ideas as she forced herself to remain in control. "Untie me," she whispered, the words sharp but confident. "I'll not cross you. Trust me, Ethan."

For a brief moment, he hesitated, the battle between trust and survival clear on his face. But there was no other choice. Reluctantly, he untied her, his hands trembling slightly. Nora stood up, smoothing down her disheveled clothes as she quickly tucked him away in the attic, ensuring he was hidden well from sight. His dark eyes bore into her as she closed the door, warning her one last time.

"If you turn on me, Doll-" His voice trailed off, but the threat was clear.

Nora smiled—a quiet, confident smile that spoke of far more than just survival. She turned away and approached the door, her steps slow and measured, as if she'd rehearsed this scene a hundred times. When she finally opened it, her face lit up with a calm, warm expression, one so convincing that even Ethan, hidden away, would have believed her innocence.

"Good afternoon, officers," she greeted, her voice carrying a gentle charm. "Is everything alright?"

The police eyed her suspiciously, one of them stepping forward. "We're investigating a missing person's report and there have been sightings of someone in this area. Mind if we ask you a few questions?"

"Of course," Nora replied, tilting her head in an act of naive compliance. "I've been staying here alone for a while now, actually. I- I'm mentally unwell," she continued, her tone softening with a believable hint of sadness. "My uncle owns this place. It's quiet here, so he lets me stay while I recover."

The officers exchanged glances, but Nora held her ground, her performance flawless. They fired off a few cross-questions, but she handled each one with ease, guiding the conversation carefully.

"You're welcome to come inside and look around if you'd like," she offered, stepping aside as if she had nothing to hide.

The two officers entered, casting glances around the cabin, but they didn't check thoroughly. They left without raising further suspicions, and as their car disappeared into the distance,

Nora released a slow breath. She'd done it. She had protected him.

Moments later, Ethan emerged from the attic, his face a mixture of disbelief and admiration. He crossed the room toward her, a twisted smile pulling at his lips. "I didn't think you could pull it off," he murmured, his voice low, but there was something else beneath it—satisfaction. "You impressed me, Doll."

Nora's eyes flicked up to meet his, a small smirk playing on her lips. "I told you to trust me."

As a reward for her loyalty, Ethan took her out to a lake deep in the woods—his usual hunting ground. The walk was silent, but there was a strange sense of peace in the air as they left the cabin behind. Once at the lake, Ethan busied himself setting traps for wild animals, looking for fresh blood.

Nora, however, wandered toward the lake, drawn to the clear blue water that shimmered beneath the sunlight. She knelt at the edge, dipping her fingers into the warm water, and without a second thought, she began to undress. Her bruised wrists, still bearing the marks of the ropes, were exposed, and as she slipped into the water, she felt an odd sense of freedom. The warmth enveloped her, soothing the aches and bruises on her skin. She submerged herself fully, her dark hair floating around her like a halo as she closed her eyes, allowing herself to savor the moment.She had never admitted it out loud, but there was a part of her that loved this—the control, the chaos, the bruises left by Ethan's hands. It was as though she was living in a twisted fantasy that she had always craved but never fully understood. She knew Ethan was hers, and only hers, no matter how dark their relationship had become.

When she finally resurfaced, wiping the water from her face, she felt a presence behind her. Turning her head, she saw Ethan standing at the edge of the lake, his eyes fixed on her with an intensity she hadn't seen before. He was silent, watching her in awe, as if seeing her for the first time.

Nora's lips curled into a teasing smile. "What?" she called out, her voice light and mocking. "You bathe me every day, Ethan. It's not the first time you're seeing me naked."

Ethan shifted, looking suddenly uneasy as his eyes darted away from her naked body. "Get dressed," he muttered, his voice unsteady. "We're leaving soon."

But Nora wasn't done playing. She stood up in the water, letting the droplets cascade down her bare skin as she turned fully to face him. "Don't be shy," she teased. "You've seen me like this more times than I can count. I thought you were the one in control?"

Ethan's jaw clenched as he stared at her, his hands tightening into fists. His discomfort grew into frustration, and before he could stop himself, he stepped into the water, fully clothed.

"You want to test me, Doll?" he growled, his voice low and dangerous. "You think this is a game?"

Nora's smile didn't waver. "Isn't it?"

The tension between them snapped in an instant. Ethan surged forward, pulling her close, his hands gripping her waist tightly as he pressed her against his chest. The heat between them was undeniable, and the frustration in his eyes had shifted into something darker, something far more primal.

Their lips collided in a heated, desperate kiss, the water sloshing around them as they gave in to the tension that had been simmering for so long. Ethan's hands roamed over her body, rough but possessive, as if he couldn't bear the thought of letting her go. Nora's hands found his shirt, tearing it open as her nails raked across his skin.

The kiss deepened, becoming more frantic, more intense. Ethan's control snapped as he pushed her back against the smooth rocks by the lake's edge, his hands gripping her thighs as he lifted her slightly. Their bodies pressed together, the water cooling the heat of their skin, but the fire between them was undeniable.

"Nora," Ethan growled against her lips, his voice hoarse with desire. "You're mine."

She responded with a bite to his lip, pulling him closer, as if to say she knew. In that moment, they were connected in every way—mind, body, soul. It wasn't just sex anymore. It was something deeper, darker, more consuming.

Ethan's movements were rough but intentional, every thrust filled with the power and possessiveness he carried. Nora's gasps mixed with the sounds of the water, her hands gripping his shoulders as she let herself fall deeper into the moment, into him. For once, she wasn't resisting. She was giving in completely.

They were lost in each other, every breath, every touch, every movement building to something raw and untamed. It was the culmination of everything they were—broken, twisted, and yet so irrevocably tied together.

When it was over, they stayed there for a moment, their bodies tangled together in the water, the world around them silent except for the soft lapping of the lake against the shore. Ethan pressed a kiss to her temple, his breath still heavy, but there was something softer in his touch now.Nora looked up at him, her eyes filled with something akin to triumph. He had her, yes—but in some ways, she had him too.

15

CHAPTER 15

Ethan had grown to trust Nora more over the weeks. The ropes no longer cut into her wrists, and though he still locked the door when he left, she was free to move around the cabin as she pleased. He would come and go, his time outside growing longer, sometimes not returning until long after nightfall.

Tonight was no different. Nora stood at the stove, stirring a pot of soup that she had managed to throw together with the sparse ingredients left in the pantry. It was late, much later than Ethan usually returned, and as the hours dragged on, a cold pit of unease settled in her stomach.

She glanced out the window at the inky blackness, barely able to see past the trees that surrounded the isolated cabin. Something felt wrong. She could sense it deep in her bones, a growing tension that made her heart race with every passing minute. Where was he?

Then, as the clock neared midnight, the door creaked open.

Nora turned sharply, her breath catching in her throat. Ethan staggered into the cabin, his silhouette illuminated only by the moonlight that filtered through the window. He was hurt. Badly.

"Ethan!" she gasped, rushing to his side. His shirt was torn and bloodied, a deep gash running across his torso, and his face was pale, too pale. He collapsed against her, his weight almost knocking her to the floor as she struggled to support him. "What happened?"

He groaned, barely able to speak. "Caught- off guard. Didn't see them coming," he rasped, his voice weak. His skin was clammy, and his breathing was labored.

Nora's mind raced as she helped him to the couch, laying him down as gently as she could. "You need a hospital," she said, panic rising in her chest. But even as she said it, she knew it was impossible. The nearest hospital was miles away, and Ethan was a wanted man. There was no way she could get him there without raising suspicion.

"No- hospital," he muttered, his eyes fluttering closed. "Too dangerous-"

She knelt beside him, her hands shaking as she pressed a cloth against the wound in his side, trying to stop the bleeding. But it wasn't enough. His pulse was weak, and his breathing was becoming more erratic by the second.

Then it hit her. She knew what he needed. Blood.

Nora had seen it before—the way his eyes darkened, the way his body weakened when he went too long without it. She knew what he was, what he needed to survive. And right now, he was dying because of it.

Without hesitating, she grabbed a knife from the kitchen counter, her heart pounding in her ears as she sat beside him. She glanced at his face, his features twisted in pain, his body trembling. There was no other option. She had to save him.

With a sharp intake of breath, she pressed the blade to her wrist and sliced. The pain was immediate, but she didn't flinch. Blood welled up from the cut, trickling down her arm in a steady stream. She held her wrist to Ethan's lips, her hand trembling as she urged him to drink.

"Ethan," she whispered, her voice hoarse. "You need this. Please, drink."

For a moment, he didn't respond, his body still too weak, but then his instincts took over. His lips parted, and he latched onto her wrist, drinking deeply from the wound. Nora winced at the sensation, but she didn't pull away. She could feel his strength returning, his grip on her arm tightening as he drank, the color slowly returning to his pale skin.

Minutes passed, and finally, when he had taken enough, he released her. Nora quickly wrapped her wrist with a makeshift bandage, her heart still racing from the adrenaline. Ethan had fallen into a deep sleep, his body no longer trembling, his breathing steady.

Exhausted, Nora slumped into the chair beside him, watching his chest rise and fall with each breath. She had saved him. For now, at least. But she couldn't shake the feeling that something had shifted between them. He had always been the one in control, but tonight, she had been the one to take care of him, to keep him alive.

It was a strange reversal of roles, and it left her feeling uneasy. She knew what he was. She knew what he needed. But she also knew that there were parts of him—dark, dangerous parts—that she could never fully understand.

As the night wore on, exhaustion overtook her, and she drifted into a restless sleep, her wrist still throbbing with a dull ache.

When Ethan woke the next morning, the first thing he noticed was the sunlight streaming through the window. The second was the dull pain in his side, the reminder of the wounds he had sustained the night before. But the most unsettling thing of all was Nora, asleep in the chair beside him, her hand bandaged tightly.

His mind raced as the events of the previous night came flooding back. He remembered stumbling into the cabin, on the verge of death. He remembered her cutting her wrist and feeding him her blood. She had known what he needed. She had saved him.

But how?

A wave of dread washed over him as he sat up, his eyes never leaving her sleeping form. How had she known? Who was she, really?

As if sensing his gaze, Nora stirred, her eyes fluttering open. When she saw him awake, she smiled softly, her expression filled with relief. "You're okay," she whispered, sitting up straighter in the chair. "I was so worried-"

Ethan's voice was cold, sharp. "How do you know?"

Nora blinked, caught off guard by his sudden change in demeanor. "What?"

"How do you know what I am?" His eyes darkened, his voice low and dangerous. "How did you know that I needed blood?"

She hesitated, her eyes flickering to the bandage on her wrist. "I- I just knew. I could see it in you, Ethan. The way you changed, the way you got weaker when you didn't—"

"Don't lie to me," he growled, cutting her off. "Who are you, Nora? Who sent you?"

Nora's heart pounded in her chest as she met his gaze. There was no fear in her eyes, only resolve. She knew this moment would come eventually. She just hadn't expected it to come so soon.

"No one sent me," she said quietly, her voice steady. "I've always known, Ethan. About you. About what you are."

His fists clenched at his sides, his mind racing. He didn't want to believe her, didn't want to accept that she had known all along. He had been careful. He had hidden his nature from her, or so he thought.

"Why didn't you say anything?" His voice was tight with anger, his hands trembling as he tried to process the weight of her words. "Why did you let me keep you here?"

Nora's gaze softened, her voice barely above a whisper. "Because I wanted to stay."

Ethan stared at her, his mind reeling. Nothing made sense anymore. But as he looked at her—really looked at her—he realized that she had always been different. She wasn't like the others, the women he had broken and discarded. She had stayed, endured, not out of fear, but out of something else entirely.

Ethan didn't know what to feel—rage, betrayal, confusion—but one thing was clear: Nora was far more dangerous than he had ever anticipated.

16

CHAPTER 16

Ethan stared at her, his chest rising and falling with a newfound fury as Nora's words settled into his mind like poison. He had been ready for anything, but nothing could have prepared him for what she was about to reveal.

"You still don't get it, do you?" Nora said softly, standing from her chair, the remnants of their dark and twisted past playing in the smirk curling at her lips. "You think all of this was your doing? That your strength, your speed, your power came from some supernatural accident?" She shook her head, stepping closer to him, her eyes gleaming with an unsettling mix of affection and something far more dangerous.

Ethan's body stiffened, his breath shallow. "What are you talking about?" His voice was a low growl, but there was a flicker of uncertainty in his tone now.

Nora tilted her head, her voice cold, distant. "You didn't become what you are by chance, Ethan. I made you."

His heart skipped a beat, the room suddenly feeling smaller, suffocating. "What?"

"I created you, Ethan," Nora continued, her voice calm but laced with a dark undertone. "You weren't always like this. You were human once. I took that from you. I took everything." Her gaze never wavered from his, the weight of her confession crashing down on him like a tidal wave.

Ethan stumbled back a step, the world spinning around him as memories he couldn't quite reach began to claw their way to the surface. "No- no, that's not possible," he whispered, shaking his head in denial. "I've always been like this—"

"You're wrong," she interrupted, her voice like a knife slicing through his protest. "You were once a man—a weak man. One that Jeffrey almost killed." She paused, savoring his confusion before continuing. "He found out about your affair with Ava, and he didn't hesitate to make you pay for it. You were dying, Ethan. Bleeding out on the floor, broken. But I—" she placed a hand on her chest, her eyes gleaming with pride, "I couldn't let you go. You were the perfect specimen."

Nora's words were like daggers, each one cutting deeper than the last. Ethan's mind raced, flashes of images he didn't understand swimming before his eyes. Jeffrey. Ava. Blood. Darkness.

"Why would you do this?" he snarled, his fists clenching, the pain in his side long forgotten. "Why?"

Nora's smirk faded, replaced with something almost tender. "Because you were perfect. I asked them to let me have you. And they did. They erased your memory, made you forget the pain, forget the weakness. But I—" she took another step closer, her breath warm against his skin, "I built something new. I gave you power. Strength. Speed. Everything you are, I made you into it."

Ethan's head was spinning, his heart hammering in his chest as he tried to process what she was saying. None of this made sense, none of this could be real. He had always been in control, always held the power in their twisted relationship. But now, now he realized he had never been in control at all. He had been a puppet. Her puppet.

"You're sick," he spat, disgust rising in his throat. "You're a monster."

Nora's face softened, but her eyes remained as cold as ever. "A monster? Maybe. But I did it for us, Ethan. For our future. I gave you everything."

"No," he said, his voice shaking with fury. "You took everything from me. You used me."

Nora's jaw tightened, the playful amusement that had colored her voice moments ago vanishing. "Used you?" she repeated, her tone sharp. "I gave you life. I saved you."

"I don't need your salvation!" Ethan shouted, his voice echoing through the cabin as he stepped back, putting distance between them. "I never asked for any of this."

For the first time, Nora looked hurt. She had always been the one in control, always pulling the strings. But now, as Ethan stood before her, the realization that she had lost him finally seemed to sink in. Her smile faltered, and she took a step back. "You don't mean that-"

"I do," Ethan growled. His eyes, usually so intense and cold, were now filled with something unfamiliar—disgust. "I could never love you, Nora. You've destroyed everything. You turned me into a monster."

Nora's face paled, the color draining from her cheeks as his words hit her like a slap. "No- I did this for us. For you. I thought- I thought you would understand."

He shook his head, his expression hardening. "You're wrong. You're sick, Nora. And I want nothing to do with you." He turned away from her, his chest heaving with a mix of rage and sorrow. "Leave. You're free."

For a moment, Nora stood frozen in place, her mind reeling from his rejection. She had spent so long believing in their twisted bond, in the idea that they were meant to be together, but now- now it was crumbling before her eyes.

"You're- setting me free?" she whispered, disbelief thick in her voice.Ethan didn't turn to face her. He couldn't. "It's over," he said, his voice low and final. "Go."

Nora's lips trembled, her hands balling into fists at her sides as she stared at the man she had created—the man who had rejected her. "I did this for you," she whispered, her voice breaking. "For us."

But Ethan said nothing.

Realizing it was truly over, Nora's breath hitched in her throat. Her fairytale—the twisted, sick fantasy she had woven around him—was over. She was free, but it didn't feel like freedom. It felt like an ending. A bitter, cruel ending.

Without another word, she turned and walked out of the cabin, leaving behind the man who had once been hers. As the door closed behind her, the weight of her creation, her obsession, crushed her. And she realized, with painful clarity, that her dream was dead.

She had lost him. And in doing so, she had lost herself.

17

CHAPTER 17

Days blurred into weeks as Nora attempted to stitch together the fragments of her broken life. She had returned to work, throwing herself into the mundane routines of the office, trying to bury the regret that gnawed at her every night. Her mind echoed with the memories of Ethan—of what she had done, how she had destroyed his life. She had created a monster, and now, she had lost him.

She walked the line of normalcy, putting on a brave face for her colleagues, but the guilt never left her. It festered in her quiet moments, reminding her of the life she had taken from Ethan—the man she had changed for the worse, even if her intentions had been warped by her obsession. Every time she looked in the mirror, she saw the face of someone who had played God, and she hated it.

Meanwhile, Ethan's world had turned upside down. After Nora's revelation, the rage he had felt began to wane, replaced by a deep curiosity and an unsettling emptiness. She had told him she created him, that she gave him this life, and though he despised her for it, he couldn't stop thinking about the past she'd referred to.

He couldn't remember much before Nora, but now, he had to know. Who had he been? What had he been before she rewrote his story?

Determined, Ethan began to trace the fragments of his old life, returning to the house he once called home—a place he hadn't visited since his transformation. The air inside was stale, heavy with dust and decay. He walked through the silent rooms, each step bringing flashes of a life that seemed foreign yet familiar. Empty whiskey bottles littered the floor, the smell of alcohol still faint in the air. The kitchen counters were scattered with pills—antidepressants, sleeping aids, anything to dull the pain.

As he ventured further, he found photographs tucked into drawers—images of himself, disheveled, eyes glazed over. His memory began to crack open, revealing pieces of who he used to be. A man living in shadows, corrupt, careless, drowning in his own vices. He was nothing more than a broken man, clinging to an affair with Ava, using her as an escape from the darkness consuming him. The nights blurred together with alcohol, and in the mornings, he was haunted by suicidal thoughts that had crept in like vultures waiting to feast.

But then- Nora.

The memory of her was sharp, clearer than anything else. She had saved him, pulled him from the brink of death, given him the strength he now possessed. Without her, he would've been gone—just another lost soul, erased from the world. But she'd given him purpose. She'd made him better, whether he wanted to admit it or not.

Ethan's chest tightened as the realization hit him. Nora wasn't the monster; she had saved him from the real monster—himself.

He couldn't stop thinking about her, the regret building inside him like a storm. She had ruined his life, yes, but she had also saved it. He had to see her again, to confront these feelings that were tearing him apart.

Driven by this need, Ethan made his way to Nora's place, his footsteps growing faster as his emotions swirled in confusion and desperation. When he arrived at her doorstep, the familiar scent of her hit him, stirring something deep within. He approached the door, hand raised to knock, but then he froze.

Through the window, he saw her.

Nora.

She was sitting on the couch, laughing at something, a bright smile lighting up her face in a way he hadn't seen in so long. But it wasn't just her. Across from her sat a man—a colleague by the looks of him, casually dressed, leaning in close as they exchanged jokes and easy conversation.

Ethan's breath hitched in his throat. Jealousy ripped through him like a blade.

Who the hell was this man? And why did he feel like he didn't belong there, watching from the shadows?

He clenched his fists, the primal need to lash out surging through him. But instead of barging in, instead of confronting her like the monster he had become, Ethan turned away. His heart pounded as he stalked back into the night, his mind racing with jealousy, anger, and confusion.

She had moved on. After everything, she had moved on.

But even as he walked away, the bitter taste of jealousy remained, and he couldn't shake the feeling that, no matter how far he tried to run from it, Nora would always be a part of him. The question that haunted him now was simple:

Had he made the right choice in letting her go?

As the rain began to fall, Ethan's mind swirled with doubt, and for the first time in a long while, he wasn't sure of anything.

18

CHAPTER 18

Ethan couldn't stop thinking about Nora, the way she laughed, the way she smiled with a freedom he had never seen before. That happiness had never existed when she was with him. The realization gnawed at him, festering like a wound he couldn't heal. It wasn't something he could shake off, no matter how hard he tried. Days passed, and he found himself lurking in the shadows, watching her from a distance, consumed by a growing obsession he couldn't control.

Every small detail about her captivated him. The way she absentmindedly tucked her hair behind her ear, the way her eyes lit up when she was deep in thought, the gentle way she spoke to her colleagues. They were things he'd never noticed when she was his, but now- now, it was like he was seeing her for the first time. And it drove him insane.

But what truly made his blood boil was that one colleague—Michael Jenkins. The man was always near her, laughing with her, talking too closely, touching her arm in ways that made Ethan's stomach churn with jealousy. Every time he saw them together, something dark stirred inside him. He wanted to tear Michael apart, to make it clear that Nora wasn't available to anyone else.

One evening, as he watched them at a distance, Ethan's heart sank when he saw Michael kneel down, his hand holding Nora's gently as he looked up at her with a hopeful expression. He couldn't hear what was being said, but the look in Michael's eyes told him everything.

Michael Jenkins was proposing.

For a moment, Ethan's world stopped. His fists clenched at his sides, and his breath caught in his throat. He couldn't lose her like this, not to someone like Michael. His jealousy burned hotter than anything he had ever felt before.

But then, to his surprise, Nora didn't immediately say yes. She hesitated, her brows furrowing as she looked down at Michael. She pulled her hand away gently and said something that Ethan strained to hear from his hiding spot. She needed time.

Time.

Ethan exhaled sharply, a mix of relief and frustration swirling inside him. She hadn't accepted the proposal, but she hadn't rejected it either. That was enough to set him on edge.

That night, when Nora returned home, she walked into her quiet apartment, her thoughts clearly weighed down by Michael's proposal. But little did she know, Ethan was waiting for her. He stood in the shadows, watching as she kicked off her shoes and sighed heavily.

He couldn't hold back his feelings any longer.

The second she walked into her bedroom, he stepped forward, his movements quiet but deliberate. Nora, startled, froze when she saw him standing there.

"Ethan?" Her voice was barely above a whisper, her eyes wide with surprise. "What are you doing here?"

Ethan didn't say anything at first. His gaze lingered on her face, the way her eyes searched his with confusion, maybe even a flicker of fear. But that wasn't what he wanted to see. He wanted to see something else in her eyes—something she had never shown him.

"You didn't accept his proposal, Doll" Ethan said, his voice low and controlled, though his heart was racing.

Nora's eyes narrowed slightly, a flicker of frustration crossing her features. "You've been watching me?"

"I couldn't stay away," he admitted, stepping closer. "Not after everything."

She shook her head, clearly torn between anger and something else. "Ethan, you don't get to do this. You set me free, remember? You let me go."

"I know Doll," he murmured, his voice rough with emotion. "But I can't- I can't pretend anymore. I've been trying to stay away, to let you live your life. But watching you with him-" He paused, his jaw tightening. "It was killing me."

Nora exhaled slowly, her gaze softening as she looked at him. "Ethan, you were the one who pushed me away. Why now?"

"Because I was wrong," Ethan confessed, his voice raw. He stepped closer until he was right in front of her, his presence overwhelming. "I thought I hated you for what you did to me. I thought I could move on. But the truth is, Nora- "

He hesitated, his eyes darkening with an intensity that made her heart race. "I can't let you go," he finally whispered. "I've fallen for you. And I don't want to fight it anymore."

Nora's breath hitched in her throat, her mind spinning with a thousand thoughts. She had never expected this. Ethan—the man she had once controlled, the man who had despised her for turning him into something else—was standing here, confessing his love for her. It felt surreal. "Ethan- " she started, but he cut her off, his voice firm.

"I don't care about Michael. I don't care about anyone else," Ethan said, his gaze burning into hers. "I only care about you. And I'm not going to stand by and watch someone else take you away from me."

Nora's heart pounded in her chest, her mind racing as she looked up at him. There was something in his eyes, something deeper than the possessiveness she had seen before. It was real this time. It was genuine. "I don't know what to say," she whispered, her voice shaky.

"Then don't say anything," Ethan replied softly, his hand reaching out to cup her cheek. "Just- stay with me. Let me prove that I can be better. For you."

Nora closed her eyes, leaning into his touch, her emotions swirling inside her like a storm. For the first time in a long time, she didn't feel like she had to run. Maybe, just maybe, they could make this work.

19

CHAPTER 19

Nora had always believed fairytales weren't for her. They belonged to other people— women with lives more interesting, with destinies written in the stars. She had never been that girl. She was just an ordinary face, a fleeting presence in a world too vast and too complicated. And Ethan? He had been her mistake. A beautiful, destructive mistake she needed to forget.

When Michael, her once good friend and colleague, had proposed, she had stood there, staring at him, her heart heavy with uncertainty. Michael was safe. He was kind, stable. But she couldn't say yes, not when her past with Ethan still lingered like a shadow over her heart. She needed time, she had told him. Time to think, to make sense of everything. She couldn't ruin another life—not Michael's, and certainly not her own.

That evening, when she returned home, her mind was a mess. She didn't know what she wanted, but she knew what she didn't want. She didn't want to be trapped by her past again, by Ethan.

But fate had a cruel sense of humor.

As soon as she opened the door, there he was. Ethan, standing in the middle of her living room like he belonged there, like he had every right to intrude on her life once more.Her heart sank. The last person she wanted to see was him. Yet here he was, as if summoned by her own regrets.

"Ethan," she started, her voice sharp with irritation, "you can't keep doing this. You don't belong here."

But what he said next shocked her more than his sudden appearance."I want you back, Doll," he said, his tone still carrying that familiar edge of arrogance, but there was something else in his voice too—something softer, regretful. "I need you. And if I can't have you willingly-" His eyes darkened with a threat, though it lacked the venom it once had. "Then I'll take you again. I'll abduct you if I have to."

Nora's body tensed, but she didn't react the way he expected. She wasn't the same woman he had once controlled so easily. Not anymore.

She crossed her arms, her expression cold. "You don't scare me, Ethan. Not anymore."

For a moment, he faltered. The usual bravado and intimidation tactics seemed to lose their power over her, and it shook him. He hadn't expected this. He had expected her to submit, to fall back into the pattern they had once lived.

"Do you think you can just come back here and say those things to me?" she continued, her voice icy. "You can't control me, Ethan. Not again."

His expression changed, the mask of indifference slipping. Desperation flickered in his eyes as he took a step closer to her. "Nora, I'm not here to hurt you. I—I can't stop thinking about you. I've tried, but nothing works. You haunt me."

She raised an eyebrow, still not letting herself soften. "That's your problem. Not mine."

"No," he insisted, his voice cracking slightly, betraying how much this was affecting him. "I- I need you. And I know I don't deserve you, not after everything. But-" He took another step forward, his hands trembling slightly. "I love you, Doll."

The words hit her like a punch to the gut. He had never said that before. Not like this.

"I love you," he repeated, his voice quieter now, almost broken. "And I'll do anything to prove it to you. I'll change. I'll be better. Just- don't push me away."

Nora stood there, her mind reeling. Ethan, the man who had once kidnapped her, tormented her, and controlled her every move, was standing in front of her, begging. It didn't feel real. It was like the world had flipped upside down.

She looked into his eyes, searching for any trace of deceit, any sign that this was another one of his manipulations. But all she saw was sincerity. Vulnerability.

"I don't believe you," she whispered, though her voice lacked conviction.

Ethan's eyes widened, panic flashing across his face. "Nora, please." He reached out, grabbing her hands, holding them tightly as if he was afraid she would slip away. "I can't lose you. I won't lose you. If you walk away now, I'll—"

"You'll what?" she interrupted, pulling her hands free from his grip. "You'll abduct me again? Lock me up until I give in? You think that's love, Ethan? Because it's not."

"I know," he murmured, his voice breaking. "I know I've been a monster. But I don't want to be that anymore. I want to be the man you deserve."

Nora's heart wavered. There was a time when all she had wanted was to hear these words from him, to feel like she mattered to him beyond his obsession. But now, after everything, could she really trust him?

"You think saying you love me makes it all okay?" she asked, her voice trembling. "You think it erases everything that happened between us?"

"No," he admitted, his head hanging low. "But I'm trying, Nora. I'm trying to be someone better. For you. I just- I need you to give me a chance."

Nora stared at him, her emotions in turmoil. Part of her wanted to walk away, to end this toxic cycle once and for all. But another part of her, the part that had once loved him—if she ever truly did—wanted to believe him.

She took a deep breath, her voice quiet but firm. "You can't just fix everything by saying you love me, Ethan."

"I know," he whispered, his eyes filled with a desperate hope. "But I'll prove it to you. Every single day, if I have to."

Nora closed her eyes, her chest tightening with the weight of the decision before her. Could she really give him a second chance? Could she trust him again?

When she opened her eyes, she saw him standing there, looking so vulnerable, so different from the man who had once controlled her life. Maybe he really had changed.

20

— ◆ —

CHAPTER 20

Nora and Ethan were back in that familiar, secluded cabin, nestled between the towering trees, where the world seemed miles away. This time, however, it felt different. The heavy tension that once filled the air had been replaced by something far gentler, more intimate. Nora was free—free to leave, to go anywhere, to live the life she wanted. But she chose to stay. Ethan loved her now, truly, in ways she had once only dreamed of, and the cabin had turned from a place of captivity to a home, their sanctuary.

Every day felt like a quiet dance of domestic life. Ethan, still hunting wild animals for blood to satisfy his dark needs, had learned to control his urges. He was careful, methodical, ensuring Nora was never in danger. He always returned to her, his expression softening the moment he stepped back into the cabin, their shared world untouched by the darkness outside.

One evening, they were curled up on the couch together, the warm glow of the fireplace casting flickering shadows on the walls. Ethan's arms were wrapped around Nora, her head resting on his chest as they watched the flames dance. It was peaceful, almost idyllic. They were connected in every possible way, more than either of them had ever imagined. But that night, something shifted in Ethan. As they lay there, his grip on her tightened just slightly, a small gesture, but enough to stir her from the comfort of their embrace.

"Ethan?" she whispered, looking up at him with a smile, her eyes full of love.

He met her gaze, but there was something wild in his eyes, something raw. The darkness in him, the very thing they had fought so hard to keep at bay, was clawing its way to the surface. He swallowed hard, trying to suppress the urge that was growing inside him.

"I need to go," he murmured, his voice strained. "I should hunt-"

Before he could pull away, Nora's hand reached up, cupping his cheek, her thumb brushing gently across his skin. "You don't have to," she whispered, her voice soothing. "Stay with me. We're safe here."

But Ethan shook his head, the hunger in his eyes growing more desperate by the second. He had never wanted to hurt her, never wanted to give in to the monster inside him. But tonight, something was different. He could feel the beast stirring, gnawing at his insides, and the more he fought it, the stronger it became.

"I can't control it," he whispered hoarsely, his breath hot against her skin. "I need to-"

Before Nora could respond, his lips were on her neck, soft at first, kissing the spot where he had kissed her before. But then his teeth grazed her skin, and she felt the sharpness of his fangs pressing against her, a warning of what was to come.

"Ethan-" she breathed, her voice trembling, but she didn't pull away. She trusted him, even now. Even when she knew he was losing control.

"I'm sorry," he whispered against her skin, and in the next moment, his fangs pierced her flesh.

Nora gasped as pain shot through her, her body tensing in his arms. His grip tightened around her waist as he drank, and she could feel the life draining from her, the strength leaving her body. She tried to push him away, but he held her close, his hunger overtaking him completely.

"E-Ethan-" she whispered, her voice weak.

Realization hit him like a shockwave, and he jerked back, eyes wide in horror as he saw the blood trickling from her neck. Nora's body went limp in his arms, her skin pale, her breathing shallow. He had almost killed her.

"No-" Ethan's voice broke, his heart hammering in his chest as he cradled her, panic flooding through him. "Doll, I'm so sorry. I didn't mean—"

But it was too late.

Tears streamed down his face as he laid her gently on the couch, frantically pressing his hand against the wound on her neck, trying to stop the bleeding. She was barely conscious, her eyes fluttering open and closed as she fought to stay awake.

"Stay with me," he pleaded, his voice shaking. "Please, Nora, stay with me. I can't lose you-"

But the guilt, the horror of what he had done, was already swallowing him whole. He was a monster. He always had been. No matter how much he loved her, no matter how hard he tried to control it, this was his nature. And he couldn't keep putting her in danger.

When the bleeding finally stopped and Nora's breathing steadied, he carried her to their bed, tucking her in gently before pressing a kiss to her forehead. She was asleep now, her body still weak from the blood loss, but alive. She would recover.

But he couldn't stay.

He wrote the note quickly, his hands trembling as he scribbled the words on the paper. Then, with one last look at her peaceful form lying in the bed, he turned and left the cabin, the door closing softly behind him as he disappeared into the night.

When Nora woke the next morning, the sunlight streaming in through the window, she reached out for Ethan, but the bed beside her was cold and empty. Her heart skipped a beat, dread creeping into her chest as she sat up, her eyes scanning the room.

That's when she saw the note.

Tears welled up in her eyes as she read his words:

I'm a monster, Doll. I almost killed you last night. I can't stay and risk your life again. I'll always love you, but I can't be with you. Please, don't come looking for me. I'm leaving to protect you. I'll always be a danger to you. I'm sorry. I'll be always look after you. Nothing can harm you, not even me. I love you Doll.

The note slipped from her fingers as she collapsed back onto the bed, her chest heaving with sobs. He was gone. Just like that, he was gone.

Her heart shattered, the pain of his absence cutting deeper than anything she had ever known. She had thought they were safe. She had thought they could be happy. But now- now, she was alone.

21

EPILOGUE

Almost five years had passed since Ethan disappeared into the night, leaving Nora with nothing but memories and a broken heart. The cabin they had once shared still stood, nestled in the woods, but now it felt different—quieter, lonelier. Nora had waited for him, holding onto hope, but Ethan had never returned.

Though her heart ached with the emptiness he left behind, she wasn't truly alone.

"Mommy, tell me about Daddy," came a small, sweet voice that brought her back to the present. Nora looked down at the little boy standing by her side, his wide, curious eyes staring up at her. He had Ethan's eyes—those deep, penetrating eyes that had once captured her heart—and his smile, the same boyish grin she had fallen in love with.

Her chest tightened as she ran her fingers through his soft hair, and for a moment, she saw Ethan in the boy's innocent face. "What do you want to know, sweetheart?" she asked softly, her voice gentle as she bent down to his level.

The boy, no more than five years old, beamed at her, his curiosity lighting up his face. "Was Daddy like me?" he asked, his eyes bright with wonder. "Did he love ad-venchu-ures? Was he strong?"

Nora smiled, her heart heavy but filled with love as she thought about Ethan. Her mind wandered back to the man who had disappeared so long ago, and though the memories were tinged with pain, she couldn't let her son know that. To him, Ethan wasn't the haunted man who had left her shattered—he was a hero.

"Your daddy was the bravest man I've ever known," she began, her voice soft and full of affection. "He was strong, stronger than anyone else, and yes, he loved adventures. He could run faster than the wind and always found his way home, no matter how far away he went."

The boy's eyes widened with amazement, his smile growing. "Did he fight bad guys, Mommy?"

Nora's smile faltered for just a moment, but she quickly recovered, nodding. "Oh, yes. Your daddy fought many battles," she said, choosing her words carefully. "But not the kind you see in stories. His battles were with himself. He was always trying to do the right thing, even when it was hard. He fought to protect the people he loved, especially you and me."

The little boy, Ethan's son, looked up at her with pure admiration, completely entranced by the story of his father. "He sounds like a hero," he whispered, his voice full of awe. Nora felt her heart clench, knowing the truth was far more complicated.

Ethan had struggled with his dark nature, his inner demons, and the terrible fear that he might hurt those he cared about. But to their son, she wouldn't let that darkness taint his memory. In her story, Ethan wasn't the monster who had run away—he was the hero who had loved her, even when he couldn't stay.

"He was," she whispered back, her voice soft with emotion. "He was a hero, my love. And he loved you so, so much."

The boy's eyes lit up again, and he giggled. "I bet I'm just like him!"

"You are," Nora said, smiling down at him. "You have his eyes, his smile, and his brave heart."

The boy beamed proudly, puffing out his chest. "Do you think Daddy will come back someday, Mommy?"

Nora's heart broke a little more at the question, and she swallowed the lump in her throat. She had told herself over the years that Ethan had left to protect her, to keep her safe from the monster he believed himself to be. But a part of her always hoped, always dreamed, that he would return. That one day, he'd walk through the door and see the boy he never knew.

"I don't know," she said softly, brushing her fingers through her son's hair. "But we'll always keep him in our hearts, no matter what."

The boy nodded, satisfied with her answer, and Nora pulled him into her arms, holding him close. He wrapped his tiny arms around her neck, and for a moment, she allowed herself to feel that hope again—the hope that maybe, just maybe, Ethan would come back.

But until then, she would make sure her son knew the best parts of his father, the parts that were worth remembering. Ethan may have been lost to his own darkness, but in their son's eyes, he would always be a hero.

As she held her little boy, Nora stared out the cabin window, her thoughts wandering back to Ethan, wherever he was. A part of her would always wait for him, but she knew now that her story had to be different. It wasn't just about waiting for a man who may never return—it was about raising the little piece of him that was still here, the boy who reminded her every day of the love she had once shared with Ethan.And so, even in his absence, Ethan lived on—in their son's laughter, in his bright eyes, and in the stories Nora told him.